To: Beata &
Daniella –

Hope you have
fun with the
book!

Yom

Z Book

Written and illustrated by Glenn G. Gauthier

Published by
Book Publishers Network
P.O. Box 2256
Bothell, WA 98041
(425) 483-3040

ISBN 1-887542-42-6
LCCN: 2006930983

10 9 8 7 6 5 4 3 2

In loving memory of my dear friend
Linda Colley

Aa

Anteater and the Artichoke

Such a funny little furry-looking
    thing was he
With a snout and tongue so long,
And beady eyes and little ears,
Somehow he looked all wrong.

He was meant to eat termites and ants,
But couldn't stand those pests.
Instead of eating all those bugs,
He liked artichokes the best!

Now whoever heard of an anteater
Who wouldn't eat an ant?
And when his mother told him to,
He said, "I simply can't!

"Some kids won't eat their carrots,
And some won't eat their peas,
But I can't eat termites and ants,
So, Mom, don't make me please!"

Bb

Bat and the bow tie

He hadn't a sock,
Not even one pair.
He hadn't a shirt,
Nor clean underwear.

Fresh out of pants,
And no pair of shoes,
He had no pajamas
To wear when he snoozed.

The one thing he had
Was a yellow bow tie.
And he wore it with pride
As he took to the sky.

Way up to the moon,
And off in the night,
Flew the little brown bat
In a yellow bow tie.

Cc

Clam on a Cloud

Down by the sea lived a clam named Sam.
He dreamed that he could fly.
He stared up above from his spot in the sand,
And he watched the clouds float by.

He would float on a cloud way above the crowd,
Down in the deep blue sea.
"I'm a clam on a cloud!" he would say out loud.
"Oh, won't you look at me!"

Then with a shake, Sam was awake,
As the tide rolled in again.
Back in the sand that was meant for a clam,
He looked to the sky with a grin.

Dragon in the dustpan

The dragon in the dustpan
Was having quite the fit,
Standing there in dirt and sand,
Trying very hard to spit.

He held his head up really high
And took a big deep breath.
Then he blew with all his might,
While puffing out his chest.

A little spark, so very small,
Was all that he could do.
Not even just one fireball.
As a dragon, he was through!

"Where's my fire? Where's my smoke?"
The little dragon moaned.
"I am nothing but a joke!
Just wait 'til I am grown!

"I'll spread my wings and fly away.
I'll leave this blue dustpan.
And then I'll blow huge fireballs,
I just know I can!"

Dd

Elephant in the egg

Ee

There is a baby elephant.
He is very small.
He lives inside an ostrich egg
That's just three inches tall.

Sometimes when this elephant
Goes to sleep at night,
He wonders if he grows too big,
The egg might get too tight.

Then he'll have to pack his trunk
And find another house.
But now he lies inside the egg,
As tiny as a mouse.

Ff

Frog and the feathers

Long ago, there was a frog named Claude.
He used to be a pollywog.
He sat like a lump. A very big clump.
He sat like a bump on a log.

He sat there and looked at the sky.
And dreamed that one day he would fly.
He said, "If I'm clever and gather some feathers,
I just might give it a try."

So he hopped off the log in the bog.
A hop is pretty common for a frog.
Then he gathered those feathers, tied them all together,
Which was really pretty clever of Claude.

Then he climbed up the biggest stump.
"I'll jump with these feathers! Yes, I'll jump!"
So he did just that. Hit the ground with a splat!
Just imagine that! What a chump!

Gg

Giant and the gumdrops

Instead of rain, the gumdrops came
From way up in the clouds.
They dropped and plopped
  an awful lot.
My word! For cryin' out loud!

Orange, green, and blue ones.
Red and yellow too.
There were so many gumdrops!
More than you could chew!

Then there came a rumble,
A tumble, and a boom.
Nine thousand pounds
  with a big huge frown
Was a giant with a broom!

He swept up all those gumdrops
And didn't share a one.
That giant with the big huge frown
Was hardly tons of fun!

Hh

Hot dog and a hula hoop

"I'm a little hot dog in a bun.
My name is Frank, and I'm very well done.
My favorite food is three-bean soup,
And I really like the hula hoop.

"I'm big for my age. I'm only three.
But I'm a whole foot long. Just look at me!
And I can dance from loop to loop,
When I have my hula hoop.

"I'll dance and jiggle, it's so much fun.
Just watch me wiggle my little bun.
I'll dance and dance until I'm pooped.
I'm a hot dog with a hula hoop!"

Inchworm and the Igloo

Just a teeny little tiny inchworm was he
And he moved real slow across the frozen sea.
It's not what an inchworm is supposed to do,
But he was very different and special too.

With a little bit of wiggle, squiggle, and flinch,
He could go real far, inch by inch.
It surely wouldn't be a cinch
To journey to the igloo.

The ice was cold on his little feet.
The wind was strong, and he felt so beat.
He bowed his head down in the sleet
On his journey to the igloo.

He traveled through the snow and hail.
His ears were ringing from the wind's loud wail.
He never thought that he could fail
As he journeyed to the igloo.

He always knew what he could do,
And he didn't stop 'til he was through.
Inch by inch and shoe by shoe
He made it to the igloo.

Ii

Kite in the Keyhole

I saw it through the keyhole,
Where light was shining bright.
I moved up close and peeked inside
And saw a wondrous sight!

Flying way up high
In a sky of pink and green,
Was a little red kite
Tugging on its string.

Looking through that keyhole
Made me want to play
On the blue and purple hill
Until the break of day.

Reaching through the keyhole,
I grabbed the little string.
But when I did I felt a tug
And woke up from my dream!

Jay with a Jewel

Jj

With a gem of a jewel in his jaw, a jay
Held that gem as he flew away.
With that shining jewel, he took to the sky,
And it sparkled in the sun as he flew up high.

With the jewel in his jaw, the blue jay soared
Way past the clouds with his just reward.
With the gem shining red and his feathers so blue,
Up, up, way up, in the sky he flew!

Kk

Ll

Ladybug and the lollipop

Looking up at me with a tiny shrug,
On my lollipop was a ladybug.
She said to me, "I love to munch
On lollipops when it's time for lunch.

"I'm sure you won't mind if I eat your treat.
I just lose control when it comes to sweets.
Could I have one more? Please don't take too long.
This lollipop I'm eating is almost gone!

"Bring me a cherry and a grape one too.
Hurry, please hurry, 'cause I'm almost through!
Yum! Yum! Yum! Crunch! Crunch! Crunch!
There's nothing like lollipops for lunch!"

Martian on a Marshmallow

Flying through the window
And landing on my nose
Was a funny little Martian
On an orange marshmallow.

As I sat there staring,
I could hardly breathe.
My nose began to tickle.
I thought that I would sneeze!

The Martian looked quite panicked
And said, "I'd better go,
Back to my planet
On my orange marshmallow."

So he flew back out the window
Right past the moon of cheese.
And to this day, I have to say,
In Martians I believe!

Mm

Newt and the Noodles

N n

"My name is Newton and I am a newt.
I think for a newt, I am really quite cute.
So maybe you'd like to take care of me.
I'll make a good pet, I'm sure you will see.

"I don't need much care, just a small place to live,
Some food and some water, whatever you'll give.
I'll make no demands. I'm not very picky.
Whatever I am, I'll never be icky!

"But one thing I'll need, and ooodles and ooodles,
Is a really big bowl overflowing with noodles!
I'll slurp them right down and chew, chew, and chew
The whole kit and kaboodle, until I am through!"

Otter and the Onion

All the little otters loved to play.
They swam and they played in the sun all day.
But Ollie the otter just cried and cried,
And none of his friends ever knew why.

He sat all alone on a rock in the sun.
He sat with his ball, but he never had fun.
All he would do is sigh and cry,
And just sat there wondering why.

Then one day he decided to play.
So he took his ball out to play in the bay.
But when the other otters swam near,
They, too, started to sniffle and tear.

They gave it their all, and they tried and tried
To play with the ball, but they cried and cried.
'Till one of the otters said, "We're so dumb!
This ball's not a ball. It's a purple onion!"

So they took the onion and threw it away.
Then they had fun for the rest of the day.
That one little guy had the most fun of all
Throwing away that dumb purple ball!

Penguin with a Pea

I opened the ice box
And what did I see?
A penguin with a little green pea.

He was black and white
And he gave me a bite,
That penguin with the pea.

He was so very nice
As he sat on the ice
Sharing his little green pea.

Who would have thought
When I looked for a pop,
A penguin I would see?

P p

Qq

Quail and the Quilt

Feeling quite bland
In just black, grey, and tan,
The quail wore a quilt on her tail.
In red, yellow, and blue,
As she stood there she knew,
She was far from looking pale.

She stood regal and grand
With a green rubber band
Holding her garment in place.
The other quails snickered,
Teased her and bickered,
And said, "You're such a disgrace!"

"Oh, stop all your chatter!
I'm feeling quite flattered
With all this attention I see.
I know that it's true,
Red, yellow, and blue
Look rather quite stunning on me!"

Rr

Robot in my Rice

There was a robot in my rice.
He sure gave me a scare.
I have to say he was not nice.
He wouldn't even share.

When I went to take a bite,
He grabbed my fork and spoon.
And flung the rice with all his might
All around the room!

Then with a clatter, splat and clink
The bowl was on the floor.
And when I put it in the sink,
The robot was no more!

Starfish in my Shoe

I pulled my two blue socks on,
Then I grabbed a shoe.
And when I put my foot in there,
I felt something move.

I pulled my foot out right away
And jumped up in surprise.
Then I looked down in my shoe.
A starfish was inside!

He said to me, "I have five arms,
And you have five of those.
How can we both fit in here
When you have all those toes?

"You'll have to move your foot now.
There is no room for two."
Then he winked and smiled at me,
The starfish in my shoe.

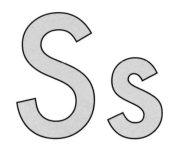

Tt

Toucan in the toaster

The toucan in our toaster
Was getting pretty hot.
Almost a crispy critter
'Til the toaster went, "pop, pop!"

Up, up from that toaster
With my toast he flew away.
He soothed his smoking feathers
And then I heard him say,

"All I really wanted
Was a little crumb of bread.
What was I thinking
In my funny bird-brain head?

"I could have gotten stuck
In that toaster on the shelf,
And might have ended up
As a piece of toast myself!"

U u

Unicorn and the Umbrella

There is a place where I have seen
A unicorn in shades of green.
He also had red polka-dots
And a huge umbrella that did not.

Yellow and blue with stripes of white
This strange umbrella took to flight,
Turned upside down and opened wide,
With the unicorn snug inside.

He floated way up in the air
Seemingly without a care,
But how he wished that he were not
Shades of green and polka-dot.

Vacuum and the Vitamins

I spilled my vitamins on the floor.
They fell and bounced on the floor galore.
From wall to wall they filled the room.
This was a job for Vic the vacuum!

So, I plugged him in and off he went,
Blowing hot air out of his back vent.
He sucked up those vitamins, A, B, and C.
And began to quiver with energy!

He sputtered and shook and stretched his long hose,
Inhaling those vitamins up his big nose!
He rolled and he raced all through the room
'Til all of those vitamins were consumed.

Finally, it seemed, he decided to rest.
He did a great job cleaning up that big mess.
And what I learned from that vacuum, I'd say,
Is to eat all my vitamins up every day!

Ww

Walrus on my Waffle

"Excuse me!" I said, to my waffle one morning,
As it moved on the plate and it gave me no warning.
I took a good look at the squares that were full,
Of blackberry syrup and syrup of maple.

I bent down and peered as close as I dared,
And I jumped in surprise when I saw what was there!
Sitting alone in one of those squares
Was a walrus on my waffle!

He looked up at me and I heard him say,
"This waffle is mine and here I will stay.
You can eat toast although it tastes awful,
So pass me whipped cream for my waffle!"

Xylophone and the X ray

"For a xylophone, I'm not sounding okay.
Something is wrong with a note when I play.
Am I sounding too sharp? Or do I sound flat?
I'm really not sure what to think about that.

"I'll visit the doctor. I may have the flu!
He'll check me right up and know what to do!
He may take an X ray of some of my keys.
Maybe the problem's the key of high C!

"Or maybe a screw or a wing nut is gone.
Whatever it is, I am sounding all wrong!
The doctor will know how to give me relief.
Then I'll sing out, with my do, re, and mi!

"I'm sure I'll sound great! I'll be okay.
Thanks to the doc and the little X ray!"

Xx

Yolk in the Yard

I looked out the window
And what did I see?
A yoke in the yard as big as could be.
I yelled to my mom,
"Quick, come and see,
This yoke in the yard that is bigger than me!"

As we stood on the porch
We kept rubbing our eyes,
Shaking our heads in total surprise!
"It's sunny side up!"
My mom finally said.
"Just how you like them for breakfast in bed.

"Go get your sister,
Your dad, and the dog.
There's even enough for Claude your pet frog."
So we all had our breakfast
To start the new day.
And when we were through, I went out to play.

Then I stood on the porch
And what did I see?
Not a yoke in the yard, just grass and a tree!

Yy

Zz

Zebra with a Zipper

Help! Help me! Someone help me!
I'm really quite a mess.
That zebra over there
Took the zipper off my dress!

My zipper's in the mouth
Of that zebra with big ears!
Oh, can you get my zipper back?
My gosh! My word! Oh dear!

How will I keep my dress up?
It's falling past my knees!
Please help me get my zipper
From that crazy zebra, please!

Can you match these pictures to the correct letters on the next page?

Aa Bb Cc Dd Ee

Ff Gg Hh Ii Jj

Kk Ll Mm Nn Oo

Pp Qq Rr Ss Tt

Uu Vv Ww Xx Yy

Zz

About this Book

Writing, illustration and design by Glenn G. Gauthier.
The illustrations were done with acrylics and colored pencil.
The text type is Nueva Std and Zipty Do and the display type is Futura.
Printed and bound by Bang Printing.

About the Author

Glenn Gauthier is an award-winning graphic designer and illustrator.
This is his debut as a children's book writer.
Glenn lives in Seattle, Washington.